ANNIE...ANYA
A Month in Moscow

story and pictures by

IRENE TRIVAS

ORCHARD BOOKS NEW YORK

Orchard Books, 95 Madison Avenue, New York, NY 10016

Manufactured in the United States of America. Printed by Barton Press, Inc.
Bound by Horowitz/Rae. Book design by Mina Greenstein.
The text of this book is set in 14 point Cochin.
The illustrations are watercolor, reproduced in full color.
2 4 6 8 10 9 7 5 3 1

Library of Congress Cataloging-in-Publication Data
Trivas, Irene. Annie—Anya : a month in Moscow / story and pictures by Irene Trivas. p. cm.
Summary: Five-year-old Annie spends a month in Moscow learning Russian words, making friends, and exploring the city.
ISBN 0-531-05452-7. ISBN 0-531-08602-X (lib. bdg.)
[1. Soviet Union—Fiction.] I. Title. PZ7.T7375An 1992 [E]—dc20 91-46433

FOR ROSE
И ТРЕМ
РУССКИМ ДЕВОЧКАМ
ОЛЯ, КАТЯ И ЖЕНЯ

WHEN Annie was five years old, she went to Russia with her mom and dad. Both of them were doctors and were invited to work in a Russian hospital for a month. They couldn't very well leave Annie behind, so they took her along.

Her dad told her that Russia was very far away and that the people there spoke Russian, not English. "That's stupid," Annie said. "Everyone speaks English. Everyone I know." She didn't much want to go, but she wasn't about to be left out of anything.

They flew on a plane for hours and hours. Annie stayed awake until she saw the North Pole. Then she fell asleep.

When she woke up, the plane was about to land in Moscow.

They were driven to a hotel in the middle of the huge gray city. Annie clutched her mother's hand very hard. She was scared. The streets were ten times wider than any back home, and the hotel seemed to go on forever.

In the hotel, Annie couldn't understand a word anyone said to her. Back home, she knew her ABCs perfectly well. In this crazy lobby, she couldn't make out a single sign. A Russian *A* was still an *A*, but the *B* was now a *V*, the *C* was an *S*, and the *H* was an *N*, for heaven's sake. Her mom tried to explain the differences to her, but Annie didn't want to know. She sang her very own alphabet song over and over again in a loud voice.

When they sat down to eat, Annie asked for her favorite sandwich, peanut butter and banana. Sadly, the waiter shook his head. Annie burst into tears. "I want to go home!" she cried. Instead, she was given some bread and butter and milk.

That night, when she went to bed, Annie's dad sang her to sleep with the alphabet song.

The next morning, they went to Red Square (which wasn't red at all) and to some dark old churches full of pictures called icons.

After a while, her dad carried her piggyback, but Annie was still grumpy. "You have jet lag," he said. That sounded like a disease, and it didn't make her feel any better.

The following day, they took the subway to go to the circus. The escalators were better than a roller coaster—they went whizzing down and down and down to the train, and then up and up and up again into the sunshine. Annie's dad got dizzy, and her mom had to squinch her eyes shut, but Annie loved it almost better than the circus.

Almost!

At the circus, Annie forgot all about icons and alphabets. She even forgot she was in Russia.

Afterward, they tried to go shopping. There were long, long lines in front of every store, but once they got in, there was hardly anything to buy.

Back in their hotel room, even the TV talked in Russian. But so far, Annie knew only two words: "da" for yes, and "nyet" for no.

"Russia is a big fat NYET!" she whispered to her doll.

Everywhere they went, people made a great fuss over Annie—especially the old ladies who patted her cheeks and called her a "krassotka." Her mom said that meant beautiful girl, and she should thank people in Russian and say, "Spassiba." But Annie didn't want to say anything. She was just plain homesick. She wanted to eat pizza and play with her best friend, Fred, and tell secrets to George, her stripy orange cat.

On their fourth day in Russia, Annie's mom and dad had to go to work. They took her to a Russian day care center and left her with Nadya, a Russian lady who smiled a lot and spoke a little English.

All the children stared at Annie. She hated them. She clutched her doll and bit her lip hard so she wouldn't cry.

Nadya led her to a table with puzzles on it and gave her a chair to sit in. But Annie wouldn't play—with the puzzles or with the children. She didn't say a word and she never smiled. She just sat and watched all that day and all the next as the children built a city with blocks.

The next time Annie came to day care, Nadya took Annie by the hand and led her to a pigtailed little girl. "This is my daughter, Anya. She was sick at home, but now she is better," Nadya said.

Anya smiled. She pointed to herself and said, "Ya Anya!" and Annie smiled a little and pointed to herself. "I'm Annie."

Anya beamed and singsonged, "Annie . . . Anya . . . Annie . . . Anya!" Then she held up her rag doll and said, "Maya kukla, Katya!"

Annie pointed to her own doll. "Kukla?"

"Da!" said Anya.

That's a funny word for doll, Annie thought. "My kukla is called Katie," she said.

Anya giggled and sang some more: "Annie . . . Anya . . . Katie . . . Katya!"

Annie couldn't help herself and she joined right in.

By the time Annie's mom and dad came to pick her up, she could say "sabaka" for dog and "koshka" for cat and "dom" for house. When Anya called out, "Dosvidanye, Annie!" Annie figured that had to mean good-bye, so she yelled back, "Dosvidanye, Anya!"

In the cab, all the way to the hotel, Annie sang a song she had made up by herself.

"Katie's a kukla,
House is a dom,
Dog is sabaka,
And George is a KOSHKA!"

She sang it over and over, and her mom and dad and the cabdriver joined right in.

After that, Annie couldn't wait to go back to day care. She went every day. She learned new words from Anya and Misha and Olga and Sasha and the other children. After all, Russian might come in handy back home. She could teach Fred the words she knew, and they'd have their own secret language.

Girls were "dyevoutchki," and boys were "maltchiki," and they were pretty much like the dyevoutchki and maltchiki at home. Even horrible Kolya, who pulled her hair and pinched her. He was just like Tommy next door.

Annie learned the word for nose,

the word for hands,

the words for eyes and ears,

and one day she called Kolya "dourak"—
the Russian word for stupid.

Every day she brought new words home to her mom and dad.

One snowy day, Nadya and Anya took Annie home with them. Anya opened the door to their apartment and said, "Maya kvartira!" They were met by a crinkly old lady and a man with a gold smile. Anya said, "Maya babushka. Moy papa."

That was easy. Papa was papa, and the old lady must be Anya's granny—her babushka.

They all sat down to tea. Babushka patted Annie on the cheek and of course she said, "Krassotka." And Annie said, "Spassiba, Babushka!"

The old lady beamed and asked her, "Gavarish po Rousski?"

"Da!" said Annie. You bet she could speak Russian. She walked around the room pointing to all kinds of things and naming every one of them: "Kniga! Kartina! Sabaka! Tchaynik! Koshka!"

Everyone laughed and clapped their hands.

On sunny days, the children were taken to the park. They climbed all over the make-believe ducks and fed the real ones.

Once they took a bus to the holy city of Zagorsk, where they were all sprinkled with holy water. Afterward, the children behaved themselves . . . for about ten minutes.

And every day after school, Annie went with Anya to Madame Olga's ballet class.

Much too soon the month was up. It was time to leave Russia and go home. Nadya invited Annie and her mom and dad to a going-away party.

Annie's parents brought Nadya and her family all sorts of presents: they gave Babushka and Nadya and Anya's father their very own boots and sweaters and gloves. Annie gave Anya her best sneakers and all her books and crayons and a whole bunch of chewing gum.

Anya gave Annie a book of Russian fairy tales, her old stuffed dog, and a Matryoshka doll that was really six dolls, one inside the other.

When everyone crowded around the little table for tea, Annie named all the food that was so beautifully laid out—"masslo," "bliny," "hlyeb," "varyennie," "tchay."

After tea, they went outside and stood in the falling snow while Annie's dad took pictures. Everyone kissed everyone else on both cheeks.

Annie and Anya hugged each other as hard as they could, and they said, "Dosvidanye," which really means, *Until we meet again*. . . .